Reading Together

Once Upon a Time

D1312265

Read it together

It's never too early to share books with children. Reading together is a wonderful way for your child to enjoy books and stories—and learn to read!

One of the most important ways of helping your child learn to read is by reading aloud—either rereading their favorite books, or getting to know new ones.

I like this story best.

Who's this over here?

It's the three pigs building their house!

Encourage your child to join in with the reading in every possible way. They may be able to talk about the pictures, point to the words, take over parts of the reading, or retell the story afterward.

Daddy's washing up. I look out. Is that someone walking about?

With books they know well, children can try reading to you. Don't worry if the words aren't always the same as the words on the page.

If they are reading and get stuck on a word, show them how to guess what it says by:
* looking at the pictures
* looking at the letter the word begins with
* reading the rest of the sentence and coming back to it. Always help them out if they get really stuck or tired.

That wolf's bow—

He's hurt his toe so he's . . .

Howling!

Sometimes you can help children look more closely at the actual words and letters. See if they can find words they recognize, or letters from their name. Help them write some of the words they know.

Wolf—it begins the same way as William and whistle.

What's happening in this picture?

Talk about books with them and discuss the stories and pictures. Compare new books with ones they already know.

We hope you enjoy reading this book together.

For Jasmine

Second U.S. edition in this form 1999

Library of Congress Catalog Card Number 92-53139

ISBN 0-7636-0858-0

4 6 8 10 9 7 5

Printed in Hong Kong

Candlewick Press
2067 Massachusetts Avenue
Cambridge, Massachusetts 02140

Once Upon a Time

conceived and illustrated by
John Prater

text by
Vivian French

CANDLEWICK PRESS

Early in the morning,
Cat and me.

Not much to do.
Not much to see.

Dad's off to work now,
Mom's up too.

Not much to see.
Not much to do.

Day's getting older,
Sun's up high.

Wave to a little girl
Hurrying by.

Mom's cleaning windows.
There's a bear.

He's making a fuss
About a chair.

Ride my tricycle
For a while.

There's an egg
With a happy smile.

Mom's in the garden,
Laundry's dry.

Why do babies
Always cry?

We've got sandwiches—
Cheese today.

Why's that wolf saying,
"Come this way"?

I like jumping
To and fro.

That wolf's howling.
He's hurt his toe.

Mom's drinking coffee
By the door.

I can jump
That far and more!

Sun's going down now
In the sky.

Here's Dad home again!
We say, "Hi!"

Dad's washing dishes.
I look out.

Did I hear someone
Prowling about?

Time for my story.
I yawn and say,

"Nothing much happened
Around here today."

Read it again

Many well-known stories and rhymes feature in the text and illustrations of this book. You may enjoy looking back through the pictures to tell the tale of each set of characters. You could also find and read the original versions of these stories and rhymes.

The Family
What happens to the little boy's cat?

The Three Little Pigs
Who wants to blow their house in?

Goldilocks and the Three Bears
Who fixes the broken chair?

The Giant
Whose tail does
he step on?

The Witch
Why does she
get angry?

Hey Diddle,
Diddle
Can you sing
the song about the
cat and the fiddle?

Humpty Dumpty
Can you say a rhyme
about him?

Little Red Riding
Hood
What
happens
to her?

Reading Together

The Reading Together series is divided into four levels—starting with red, then on to yellow, blue, and finally green. The six books in each level offer children varied experiences of reading. There are stories, poems, rhymes and songs, traditional tales, and information books to choose from.

Accompanying the series is the *Reading Together Parents' Handbook,* which looks at all the different ways children learn to read and explains how *your* help can really make a difference!